The Making of A Killer

I0460336

Andy Grossman

Copyright © 2015 Benebula Records

ISBN-10: 0692532595

ISBN-13: 978-0692532591 (Benebula Records)

DEDICATION

To my children, Monica and Benjamin who have always inspired, encouraged and motivated me.

CONTENTS

ACKNOWLEDGMENTS

This book would not have been possible without the urging of my son, Benjamin Grossman, of Benebula Records Publishing, to write it. Thank you, Son, for believing I had a story to tell and publishing it for me. Also, I want to acknowledge my wife, Julie, for proof reading, encouraging me and being my partner as we explored many of these Ghost Towns that are mentioned in the story.

Author's Note

As a young boy I remember my father taking me too many Ghost Towns in Montana such as Diamond City, Confederate Gulch, and Virginia City. Later in life when I lived in Nevada and California I had the privilege to visit Lucky Boy, Bodie, Aurora, Candelaria, Marietta, Rhyolite, Goldfield, Tonopah and many more Ghost Towns. The towns you read in this story existed at one time or another. The travel directions are as accurate as I could make them. You will find woven in the story some of my experiences and passions with such things as identifying common plants with edible and medicinal properties, shooting a hand gun, emergency preparation and dealing with Post Traumatic Stress Disorder. My hope is that you may learn something helpful as you are being entertained. By the way, all the people in the story are fictional.

CHAPTER 1

The sky was blue bird blue and a touch of a gentle breeze softly caressed the aspen trees as Jake shoveled out the barn for the last time. Tomorrow was the big day. The family was leaving the Minnesota homestead and headed to California. Uncle Dan had been there and said it was the most beautiful country in the world. Gold nuggets lay in the creek beds for anyone to pick up. There were lush, green valleys that anyone could homestead. If you liked to farm at a lower elevation you could claim some of the fertile lowlands. If you liked to get up a little higher there were foothills with seeps and springs that made ranching a dream. If you liked the mountains there were huge valleys just waiting for someone to lay claim to them and build them up.

If you liked trapping – well, the mountains were filled with beaver, elk, deer and bear. Besides that – there were no bugs like Minnesota had. You could sit around the campfire and not have to swat flies and mosquitos. Winters were mild and summers were nice. It seemed like heaven to little Jake.

Uncle Dan was known to exaggerate a mite but he could sure paint a wonderful picture with words. Jake remembered the first night Uncle Dan got back from his travels out west. They stayed up late listening to him tells stories of the wild west. His words were so colorful they sparked the imagination. Jake could see the stream beds glistening with gold and the farms with cultivated crops. He could see the fierce Indians with war paint, bows and arrows and feathers in their hair. There were lands of the Sioux they would have to travel through, then the Utes and Paiutes and Shoshone and who knew what other tribe waited to hinder their quest.

Jake wasn't scared. There were a lot of Chippewa Indians in Minnesota and they didn't bother people much. He didn't think these other Indians would give them too much trouble, either. If they did Uncle Dan and Dad would take care of them. Neither one was very big but both had been through the war. People who knew them treated the brothers with a lot of respect. The brothers joined the Eighth Wisconsin, Independent Battery when the war first started. They were among the few survivors of the bloodiest battles of the War Between the States.

Uncle Dan must have gotten through to Jake's Dad with all his tall tales because it didn't take long for him and his Mom to decide to sell out and head west. Maybe it was the stories Uncle Dan told or maybe it was the farm. Conditions had been tough the last few years and it was hard to stay ahead of the bills. Their neighbor, Jeb Jones, had been ready to buy the farm as soon as they put it up for sale. Now they had the supplies they needed to head west with a little left over for a new start.

Jake and his older brother, James, were so excited that they could hardly stand it. Jake, being ten years old and small for his age, looked up to his brother, James, (who was 14). James protected him at school and helped with chores and was the most wonderful brother anyone could have. Once in a while they had their skirmishes but mostly they got along really well.

"Hey, James!" Jake yelled. "Are you ready to go start a new life in California?"

"Sure, Jake." James replied, "But we might go to Oregon, ya know. Oregon is a right nice place, too."

"I don't care where we end up," Jake said. "Just as long as it is somewhere else."

"I want to see something new. I want to see those 'Shining Mountains' Dan talks about. I want to find a stream with gold nuggets!"

"Jake, I think you are swallowing some of Uncle Dan's fairy tales." James said smiling. It's been over twenty years since the gold rush. The old trapping days are mostly over, too."

"Besides," James said, "Pa and Ma and I want to go where we can stake out our own homestead and raise cattle or grow crops. There is where the real gold is."

So it was that the King family, Jake, James and mom and dad, (Mary and Andrew,) packed what they could in their newly purchased Conestoga wagon, pulled by three teams of oxen, headed where the sun set with great dreams and aspirations.

Actually, they had to go mostly south to Weston, Missouri to meet up with a wagon train before they could actually travel west. But nothing could dull their enthusiasm on that bright spring day. They were off and their destination was west toward the setting sun!

Jake thought of the beautiful sunset of the previous evening. As it slowly settled in the western sky it colored the horizon with a golden glow that seemed to indicate that there was a golden future for him that lay in that direction.

As the oxen settled into their routine, Jake liked to spend some time with Uncle Dan. Sometimes Jake would crawl up behind Uncle Dan and ride with him. Dan pointed out the plants that were edible or had medicinal qualities. Of course he was familiar with dandelion and they used chicory root to add to their coffee, but it seemed like every plant was valuable for something. Uncle Dan said that a person need never go hungry if he knew plants. Of course there were poisonous ones, too. So it was important to tell the difference between a good plant and one that could kill you.

Jake learned that Plantain, lambs quarter and mallow, plants that he had seen all his life, were good to eat. Purslane, Milk Thistle and cattail were also plants he was familiar with but never thought of eating. When he could he would gather some plants up and his mother would cook them with dinner. Most were pretty tasty with a little salt and butter on them. Most were pretty bland or even a little bitter – but so were a lot of the vegetables from the garden. That's why Mom spiced them up or made a dressing for them.

Jake learned that yarrow was good to eat or you could boil it for a tea which would relieve congestion in the lungs. It was also a pain reliever and could help stop bleeding. As they rode along Dan would point out a plant like mullein that was easy to identify and ask Jake what it was good for.   After a few weeks, Jake was pretty good at identifying plants and knowing what their good qualities were. He also learned to identify the bad ones.

On Sunday the family would take the day off and have church. Jake loved to sit around the fire as Dad read from the old family Bible. Mom would lead in some hymns and everyone would sing their hearts out. Uncle Dan would tell Bible stories in such a colorful way that Jake could almost see the three Hebrew children in the fiery furnace and Daniel in the lion's den. When he told the story of Joseph and how his brothers wanted to kill him but sold him into slavery instead, he almost cried. He was so glad he had such a wonderful family and brother.

On Sunday Jake got to go fishing or hunting with Uncle Dan. Uncle Dan taught him how to shoot a rifle. When he was with the Eighth Wisconsin he was a sniper and it seemed to Jake like Uncle Dan could shoot anything he could see.

"Jake, never point a gun at anything you don't want to destroy." Dan said.

If Jake forgot and let the barrel wander he got a swift kick in the rear or his old hat swatted off, by a grinning Uncle. He learned very quickly to watch where he pointed the barrel. He learned to look beyond the target or whatever he was shooting at to see where a missed shot might go. He learned to keep his finger off the trigger until he acquired his target and gently but quickly squeeze the trigger. He learned to take a breath in and hold it while he waited to shoot between heartbeats. It wasn't long before he was bringing in rabbit and then deer and antelope to put in the pot.

Supper was usually whatever meat they could kill and whatever herbs and plants they could gather to go along with the dried food they had in supply. Carrots and potatoes lasted for quite a while. Mom would put everything in a big old cast iron pot and cook it for hours. She often cooked the next day's meal and they ate the food she had cooked on the fire the previous night. It was so good and tender and flavorful. When Mom dropped some dumplings to cook with the stew, Jake's mouth watered in anticipation. Mom smiled as he ate and said he wouldn't be small for long the way he ate. Jake couldn't help it. Mom was such a great cook. The food was always plentiful and good.

As the family left the old farm and headed west, the days were warm, the grass was green and plentiful and life was pleasant. Jake's dad would often put his arm around him and show him the hand of God in the things He had made. He quoted the 19th Psalm from the Bible, "The heavens declare the glory of God; the skies proclaim the work of His hands. Day after day they pour forth speech; night after night they reveal knowledge. They have no speech, they use no words; no sound is heard from them. Yet their voice goes out into all the earth, their word to the ends of the world."

Then Jake's dad would show him some interesting plant that clearly showed design or he would point out the stars in the sky and talk about God.

Sometimes Andrew would put his arm around Jake and tell him he loved him and was so proud of him. He told Jake that he believed Jake would grow up to be a great man someday.

Jake's chest would puff out and he would feel so proud. He knew his mom and dad loved him. He knew James and Uncle Dan loved him. It made a boy feel pretty good. Life was pretty good for a Minnesota boy of ten.

Things changed pretty rapidly when they met up with the wagon train they were to join for the rest of the trip.

CHAPTER 2

It was late afternoon when the King

family crested the hill and looked down

on the wagon train near Weston,

Missouri. The prairie seemed covered

with wagons. They looked like sailing

ships in a harbor to Jake. Someone said

that was the reason some people called

them schooners.

There were big Conestoga wagons

like theirs and smaller prairie schooners,

farm wagons and variations of every

kind. They all had canvas tops and many

had awnings. Pots and pans and barrels were tied around each one. Barrels were filled with flour, rice, beans and everything under the sun. Each wagon had at least one barrel for water.

Some people had set up tents for their little village. People of every description were running around like ants on an ant pile. One of the tents seemed to be the center of activity and Andrew King headed for it.

When he got as close as he could he hopped off the wagon and went in search of the Wagon Master. He found out that big Sam Logan was the Wagon Master. When he found him he paid his fee and got the rules for the wagon

company. Part of rules or articles as

they called them were:

Rule 1- The Wagons shall be

capable of bearing one fourth more than

their load, and the Teams able to draw

one fourth more than their load.

Rule 2 -The number of Loose Cattle

shall never exceed 33 to one driver.

Rule 3 - No ardent spirits shall be

taken or drank on the route except for

medicinal purposes, and if smuggled in

shall when discovered be destroyed

under the control of the Commandant.

Rule 4 - Each male over the age of

sixteen shall furnish himself with a good

and sufficient gun and one and a half pounds of powder and 6 pounds of lead to be inspected and reported on as in other cases.

Andrew King received directions on where to camp for the night and headed toward that area.

Their camp spot wasn't too far from the river so they filled their water barrels and found level ground and began to make camp for the night.

"Hey, Mom!" Jake said, "Can I go explore?"

"Sure, Son. Just be back in time for dinner."

As Jake walked around the camp he could feel the excitement of the people. Most were excited about starting a new life in a new land. Like the Kings, they had sold farms, businesses, and homes to pursue a dream. They had heard that the loam in Oregon was ten feet deep. They had heard the water was sweet, pure and plentiful. They heard all kinds of stories to excite them and give them hope for a wonderful future.

Some were running away. He heard some were leaving parents and hometowns to make it on their own. Some were leaving mates that were too constricting, controlling or abusive.

There were a few that were fleeing the

law. They were in trouble back home

and the west held promise of escape

from the consequences of crimes

committed. The feeling Jake got, as he

toured through the camp, was one of

hope and freedom. Everyone was eager

to start a new life.

As Jake came to the edge of camp

he spied a group of kids about his age.

One, who was a little bigger than the

others, seemed to be in charge.

"Well, look what we got here,

boys!" The big kid sneered when he saw

Jake.

Ten pair of eyes turned to look at Jake. Jake smiled and said, "Hi, guys! I'm Jake King. What are your names?"

A few kids smiled and were ready to speak but the big kid butted in and snapped. "Who told you to talk, Jake the snake? Nobody told you to speak!"

"I didn't mean to butt in," Jake replied, I'll just be on my way. I don't want any trouble."

"Well, you got trouble, you little shrimp!" The older boy jumped off the log he had been sitting on and strolled over to Jake. Without warning he punched Jake in the nose and knocked him down.

"What did you do that for?" Jake said. "I didn't do anything!"

"I don't like fools to butt into my business! Snakes need to be stomped!" The bully sneered as he hit Jake again. Jake jumped up and took a swing at the bigger boy. The bully laughed and hit Jake again. Jake charged him but the boy shoved him down. He then started to kick Jake, laughing as Jake tried to roll away.

"Stomp the snake! Stomp the snake!" The mean kid shouted.

A few of the boys joined in kicking Jake.

Jake curled up into a ball and tried his best to protect himself. A few kicks got in but he didn't get hurt too badly. After a while the game lost interest to the brute and he walked away. "Come on, guys! Let's get outta here."

As Jake got to his feet, trying to hold the tears back, a girl about his age came out of the bushes and helped him pick up his hat and brush off.

"Who are you?" Jake asked with trembling lips.

"I'm Amy. That big bully is Martin Bigelow. We call him Mean Martin. He bullies all the kids. If you don't do what he wants he picks on you. He is really mean and sneaky, too."

"Why?" said Jake. "I didn't do anything to him."

"It doesn't matter!" Amy said. There is something wrong with him. He likes to hurt people. He likes to hurt animals, too. It is almost as if he get pleasure out of other people's pain. I saw him stomp a puppy to death one time. The poor thing wandered away from someone's wagon. Martin made sure he never found his way home. It was horrible! The puppy was crying; I was crying and it only made Martin laugh!"

The next few weeks were a living hell for Jake. Whenever he got around Martin and tried to make friends with the other boys, Mean Martin would do something to hurt him. One time the kids were sitting around the campfire and Martin took a burning stick and burned Jake on the neck.

"Oh, I'm sorry! It was an accident!" Martin said with a fake look of remorse.

Jake had to watch where he was because Martin would trip him when Jake's arms were full of firewood or he was carrying pails of water from the river. He thought about telling his big brother, James. But he didn't want to be a baby. He had to learn to take care of himself.

"Jake!" Mom said one evening. "What is going on with you? You aren't eating and you are jumpy as a cat in a room full of rocking chairs." She tried to give him a hug but Jake evaded her arms.

"Nothing, Mom! I can take care of myself!" Jake blurted out with a hurt look.

Andrew and Uncle Dan looked at each other with a knowing look in their eyes. A little later Uncle Dan walked up to Jake. "What's going on, Son? You look like you are carrying the weight of the world on your shoulders."

"Nothing, Uncle Dan."

"Come on, buddy. Something's going on and I want you to tell me about it NOW!" Uncle Dan insisted.

Jake could not hold it in any longer. He confessed that he was being bullied by Mean Martin Bigelow and told Uncle Dan what was happening.

"I thought it was something like that," Uncle Dan said. "Well, I guess it's time to learn a few things to protect yourself."

"I can't do that!" Jake said, "He is way bigger than me!"

"Sometimes that can be a disadvantage," Uncle Dan said. "You see, you have to see an enemies weaknesses as well as his strengths. Sometimes what seems like strengths can be used to work against a man."

"See that old man over there?" Uncle Dan asked, as he looked at Jakes dad over by the fire.

"You mean Dad? Jake asked.

"Yes." Jakes uncle replied. "That average sized man beat a man half to death that was twice his size when we were with the Wisconsin battery. This big ol' boy started picking on, what he thought was a mild mannered little guy.

Only this little guy was your dad and the big ol' boy made the mistake of thinking meek and mild was weakness."

"What happened?" Jake asked with big eyes.

"You Dad took a lot. He let the scoundrel push him around quite a bit. He did everything he could to avoid a fight."

"What happened then, Uncle Dan? Jake asked excitedly.

"That ol' boy push once too often! He done crossed the line! Why your Dad was all over that boy like white on rice. Every time the bully swung at him your Dad easily ducked and hit him in the ribs. That ol' boy was BIG! But he wasn't as fast or as knowledgeable about fighting as Andrew was. That big luge would take a wild swing at your Dad and when he swung around past him he got a punch that came from the boot straps. It didn't take too many hits like that before the guy was open and vulnerable. He ran at your Dad and tried to close with him and crush him in a bear hug. Your dad met him, only he was smaller and crouching down as well. Guess what happened?" Dan asked.

"I don't know! WHAT HAPPENED?" Jake asked excitedly.

"It's the law of physics." Dan said smiling. "When a big mass gets going it can't stop quickly. It has to continue in the direction it started. That ol' boy was big as a house. He had shoulders as wide as a barn door. When your Dad crouched down, the ruffian, top heavy, went over the top of him and your Dad snapped up and flipped him right over the top. He landed in the dust on his back with a plop. He made the mistake of trying to get up. As he did he left his chin wide open. I think that punch started from the ground. When your dad's fist hit him under the chin it flipped that bully right off his feet and onto his back!"

"He wasn't any problem to anyone after that. He had to sip soup through a straw for a month, too!" Dan said with a laugh.

"Uncle Dan! Uncle Dan! Could you teach me how to fight like that?" Jake asked excitedly.

For the next few weeks, every night and every Sunday, Jake and James learned how to protect themselves. Uncle Dan and their Dad took turns showing them how to wrestle, box and use throws. Since they were just average size they learned how to use a person's size and weight against them. They learned about speed and leverage and how to get power in a punch. They learned how to get someone in an arm bar or some other hold to make them submit or get hurt real bad.

Jake had a chance to try what he learned when he ran into Mean Martin Bigelow when he was out gather firewood.

"What's going on, Little Man?" Martin taunted. "I hear you are learning to fight! Let's see what you learned!" he said as he took a swing at Jake.

Jake swung with his forearm and caught Martin's swing and directed it harmlessly pass him. "You shouldn't have done that Martin!" Jake said.

Martin's eyes widened and he took a round house swing to smash Jake into the ground. But Jake ducked and swung a short power punch that came from his hips and back and legs. His arm only traveled a foot, but power came from his legs as he snapped up from his crouch and his back provided the power behind the punch.

The punch caught Martin right under the arm and everyone could hear ribs breaking. Mean Martin collapsed into the dust and started crying. He was done fighting.

Everyone looked in wonder and surprise with mouths wide open. Everyone was speechless. They never thought they would ever see that happen to Mean Martin.

In the month on the trail after that the kids flocked around Jake. There was a great relief; a sense of freedom and safety after the fight. The kids could go fishing and play their games without looking behind them with fear. Jake made a lot of friends. Caleb and Nate and he were inseparable. He taught them a few of Uncle Dan's tricks. They were continually wrestling and boxing and learning more and more skills.

Mean Martin was not mean anymore. He pretty much kept his distance from the rest of the kids and stayed close to his wagon. From time to time Jake would feel Martin's hot eyes on him. He seemed to be smoldering with hate.

CHAPTER 3

Life grew pretty tedious for Jake after the wagon train left Weston, Missouri. The train pretty much followed the Platte River at first. Later they followed green valleys and streams and brooks. The oxen, cattle and horses needed the water and grass.

The Platte, it was said, was "too thin to plow and too thick to drink". It was usually very shallow and wide. Once it a while it would get four or five feet deep but it was mostly sandy and muddy. The travelers had to let it settle before they could drink it. Some put a

little cornmeal in it to help clear it up.

But after a while Jake got used to it. It

sure wasn't like the clear cold water in

Minnesota but it was wet. Sometimes

that is all you could ask.

Everyone walked beside their

wagon or rode horses. Riding in the

wagon was very unpleasant. It was so

bumpy that even if you sat on pillows it

made your back ache and your head feel

like it was going to explode! Men,

women and children of every age walked

along the pace that the oxen would set.

Any dung or wood they found they would

throw in the canvas hanging under the wagon bed for fuel for the eating meal.

Usually they travelled no more than fifteen miles a day. Sometimes they would have to follow single file but usually the wagons would travel side by side to keep from eating their neighbors dust. Often they would scare up bison, deer and small game that was in their path. The hunters would then run after them. That was dinner on the hoof or paw, as the case may be.   Often Jake would be the one who made the kill, probably because he had his dad's old Springfield Model 1861. Those Henry's that most carried were weak, even though it was a big .44 caliber. It just didn't have the distance Jake had. The Spenser's weren't much better. Jake was zeroed in at 100 yards and could flip his sight up for 300 yards or 500 yards. He only had one shot but he could reload in seconds. He seldom needed a second shot, though. Some of the men hated to be out shot by a ten year old boy but Jake had a natural gift with some good training to go with it.

Jake hated to kill anything but it was a part of life. He believed God made all life and he hated to take life of any kind but they needed to eat so he steeled himself against his emotion and made the shot. Whoever made the kill shared it with his friends. There wasn't time to make jerky out of the meat so they cooked as much as they could and gave the rest away. Needless to say, the Kings made a lot of new friends.

Every chance Jake and James got they practiced new techniques and new moves on each other that either Dad or Dan taught them. They also did some target practice with their rifles. Dad and Uncle Dan had been snipers of some kind in the war and they really knew how to shoot. The boys learns a lot from them.

Jake felt himself growing bigger and stronger. His clothes all seemed to be too tight. He felt like he was getting faster and faster in his moves as well. As he sparred with his older brother he didn't have to think about what he was going to do – it just happened.

Once in a while one of the other boys would spar with him or James but usually they were so much better that the other boys refused to fight with them. Occasionally Jake would catch Martin Bigelow watching him slyly from far off. He often wondered what Mean Martin was up to. He knew something evil was cooking in that little brain of his.

It was just after a late spring rain storm that James decided to get a little meat for the pot. They were getting low and Dad didn't see any harm in letting his fourteen year old son go hunting by himself. Some fourteen year olds were the head of their families in the train. Fourteen was man age on the prairie. Every boy knew how to shoot pretty well.

James took off trotting toward a line of green trees near the horizon. He thought there might be a good chance to scare up a buffalo or a deer. Jake had the chore of collecting buffalo chips and sticks for the fire.

As James got near the waterhole, he got on his knees and started a stealthy crawl to see what he could see.

Suddenly a flock of crows rose up in a noisy roar about fifty feet ahead. He peeked up ahead and saw someone had beat him to the waterhole. He heard a shot and then something thrashing in the brush up ahead. Whoever shot must have got something!

James stood up and yelled 'hello'. As he got closer he saw a bison kicking his life out. He heard someone coming through the brush and was about to say, "good shot!" He saw it was Martin Bigelow and muttered, "Oh, it's you."

"Yup! It's me," Bigelow said with a leer on his face. "Good to see you, James. I was hoping to see Jake out here but you will do." All of a sudden the big Spenser when off in his hand. James felt a blow to his chest. He was knocked backwards onto the ground. He had a puzzled look on his face; his eyes dilated and his breath expelled for the last time in his young life.

Martin looked down at the dead boy and said sarcastically, "Oh, I'm so sorry! I tripped and my gun went off!"

He hid his glee when some of the men from the wagon train came running up to see who shot what. It was hard to do but he put on a sad face and wailed and appeared very upset to the other men. They patted him on the back and tried to comfort him because of the terrible accident.

The King wagon was in grief. Dad had to stop Jake from taking his gun and looking for Martin Bigelow. "It was an accident, Son. Accidents happen. Everyone said Martin was so broken up."

Jake said bitterly, "I don't care what he said or what the evidence is! I know in my heart that Martin Killed James."

"Jake! Jake! I know you are hurting but we don't have any proof of that," Dad said sadly. "I know you lost a brother, but I lost a son. I don't want to lose another one."

Jakes mother came over and put her arms around him and they both wept sadly. As the sun came up after a sleepless night, they wrapped James in a blanket and buried him in a lonely grave beside the Oregon Trail as so many others had done before them. Uncle Dad read some Scripture and Andrew King said some nice words about what a fine son James was. Mrs. King leaned against Jake and wept softly. The men and boys helped to shovel the grave in. Jake put up a cross he had made but he knew it wouldn't last long. He burned "James King" on the cross piece. He didn't have room for his date of birth and death.

Sam Logan said accidental shootings were common among the wagon trains. The jostling of the wagons mixed with loaded firearms without safety locks resulted in many accidental discharges. Inexperienced hunters and guards also shot many innocent people accidentally. Some would fire indiscriminately toward animals and any suspicious sounds outside of the wagon circles at night, which sometimes resulted in accidental shootings of friends. So James King's killing was quickly forgotten but the rest of the wagon train and chalked up to another accident. But Jake didn't forget. In his heart he knew Martin Bigelow had purposely killed his brother.

His Dad said, "No one gets away with anything, Son. We reap what we sow. If you are right and Bigelow killed James then God will punish him – if not in this life then at the Great Judgment Day. Let it go, Son."

But James couldn't let it go. He didn't forget and he didn't forgive.

CHAPTER 4

Jake dumbly set into a routine of
gathering water and firewood and doing
the little chores around camp. He
seldom went hunting. He was too angry
to have a gun in his hands. Every night
he would lie awake for hours thinking of
his big brother and the things they did
together. He remembered how James
always protected him as a little kid; how
he helped with Jakes chores when Jake
got tired; and how they would have so
much fun fishing and hunting. He sure
missed his big brother. It was hard to

believe that he would never see James again. He vowed to himself that when he got bigger he was going to look Martin Bigelow up and force the truth out of him.

Jake wasn't the only one to lose someone they loved. People died of disease, sunstroke, old age or frailty. They died of accidents, pneumonia, fevers, heart attack and in childbirth. It was a long trip over hazardous conditions. Anything could happen and it often did.

It was getting to be late spring when Jake heard they were nearing the end of Nebraska Territory. In a few days the men said they would be able to see Chimney Rock. It was a huge dome rock that had a pole like rock that jutted out of the middle of it. It could be seen for miles before they got there. Someone said it looked like a haystack with a pole sticking out of the middle.

Sometimes people carved their names on it with the date they were there. Jake decided he would carve James' name on it. He would climb as high as he could and carve his brother's name. It would be a wonderful tombstone for his brother. He would put his birth date and the day he was killed, too.

Uncle Dan often stopped by when Jake was off by himself. He asked Jake about what he thought happened and how he felt about it. He asked what Jake saw and heard that made him think that Martin killed his brother.

Just the telling of it seemed to ease Jake's aching heart. After unloading his anger and frustration on Uncle Dan he felt a lot better. Dad started every day gathering the family around the fire before breakfast and reading a chapter from the Bible and saying a brief prayer. He said it was like setting the rudder down on a sailboat. It got them off in a good direction for the day. Jake listened but there was an anger in his soul that nothing seemed to touch. Mom would hug him and tell him she loved him and Dad would put his arm around him and encourage him but James still wasn't there. His big brother's death took the joy out of his day and he continued to grieve.

Jake saw Chimney Rock and it took them two days to get to it. When they stopped for the night he and Uncle Dan rode Dan's horse to it and Jake climbed as high as he could and carved "James King" and the date he was born and the date he died in the rock. He felt better.

James would never be forgotten as long as he lived and that rock spire remained.

Jake began to hear stories of Indian attacks. The further west they went the more the stories flowed. It seemed that somebody had done something to the Indians and they were as mad as hornets. In fact, to Jake it seemed to be like when you kick a hornet's nest and they all swarm out and attack you. Dad said the Indians were the same way. As long as people left them alone they were friendly but if someone did something to rile them up – look out! They were riled up now.

Spring was flowing into summer and the wagon train left Nebraska and the Platte and soon came to Fort Laramie. The fort was in an uproar about the Indians being on the warpath. Jake and the other kids stared in awe at the colorful soldiers dressed in blue with bright yellow scarfs. The way the soldiers marched and saluted and carried themselves fascinated the boys and set more than one girls heart aflutter!

Lt. Colonel David Ranger, Commandant of the fort, cautioned the train that if they continued it was at their own peril. The troopers could only cover so much territory. The wagon train voted to continue on anyway and, fortunately, they didn't experience any problems. Independence Rock was soon in view.

Jake learned that Independence Rock was so named because a wagon train had to be there by July fourth or they would be late and took a chance of being caught in the mountain snowstorms. They seemed to be right on schedule. Everyone breathed a sigh of relief!

Things went pretty smoothly for days at a time. There was plenty of water and feed for the cattle and soon they were at Fort Bridger. They heard more stories of Indian unrest, settlers being attacked and killed, wagon trains destroyed and individuals disappearing.

It was soon after Fort Bridger that a division sprang up in the camp. Some people wanted to take the northern route and other's thought that the southern round was best. The King family decided to go with the group headed south to California. Jake was not happy to see that the Bigelow family was a part of their group.

It was as they were traveling along the Humboldt River that they were attacked. The Indians seemed to come out of thin air as they attacked. The first volley blew Jakes mom off the wagon seat. Jake couldn't believe it. He stood in shock – to numb to even think of his own safety. He and his Dad ran to Mary's side. The front of her dress was covered with blood from a large caliber bullet. Blood trickled from her mouth.

As Andrew lifted his wife's head into his arms she looked into his eyes and whispered, "Andy, it's been a wonderful life with you. I will love you forever."

Mary's head and body went limp as she exhaled into her husband's face.

"NO! NO! NO!" Jake cried. He threw himself on top of his mother and wept unconcerned and unaware of what was happening.

Jakes father gently lifted him up and said, "Jake, she isn't gone. We will see her again. She will be waiting for us. Now, go get a blanket from the wagon so we can cover her up.

Jake didn't even notice that bullets were flying by his head. They sounded like bees but he didn't care. He numbly walked to the wagon and got a blanket and draped it over the kindest, most wonderful person in the world.

Suddenly, his painful grief turned to anger. He ran once again to the wagon, got his rifle and lay across the wagon tongue and began to fire as fast as he could. Uncle Dan was standing behind the front wheel leaning across the seat of the wagon shooting as well.

Soon their firing seemed to be turning the tide. Some of the Utes began to drift away. Dan stood up for a final shot when something struck him a tremendous blow in the back. He twisted around as he fell to see what happened. He saw Martin Bigelow across the camp with smoke curling from his rifle. A leer was on his face as he ducked behind his wagon.

Jake looked down and saw his uncle fall. He knelt down next to him and lifted his head in his arms. Uncle

Dan looked into his face and stammered,

"Big…Big…" and then passed out.

"I will be a big boy, Uncle Dan! I

will be big!" cried Jake.

The bullet almost cut Dan's

backbone in half. He lived for a few

hours but he was paralyzed. He could

neither move nor talk. Sometimes it

seemed like he was trying to say

something but no one could make out

what it was.

CHAPTER 5

It was just Dad and Jake now. James,

Mom and Uncle Dan were gone. Theirs

was not the only family to lose members.

One family was completely wiped out due

to cholera. Another family lost the father

when he was kicked in the head by a

horse. The mother and children did their

best to keep up but it was difficult.

Other people's tragedy did not

relieve the King families pain, though.

Jake tried to be brave for his father. He

did his chores and helped cook and did

whatever he could. Dad still read his Bible every morning and prayed but Jake's heart was not in it. There seemed to be a coldness in his heart that wasn't there before. A smolder anger was burning in his soul.

The wagon trail turned dry and everyone carried as much water as they could. The big Conestoga wagon was no longer an asset. They choose it because they could carry a lot of furniture and things to build their home when they got to California. Now the heavy wagon cut into the dry alkali dust of the trail. Eventually they got to a place called Big

Meadows and rested up with the rest of the wagons.

Jake carried water and filled all the barrels he could preparing for the hardest part of the trip. They called it "The Forty Mile Desert". There was no water at all. The ground was sandy and difficult even for lighter wagons to get through. The wagon master, Sam Logan, decided that they would leave in the evening. That way they could cross the worst of it at night. It was every man (or wagon) for himself. If you bogged down or broke down no one would stop for you. You were on your own.

Jake had a feeling of doom. He couldn't shake the gloomy fear he had. He said, "Dad, let's wait a few days before we start."

"We can't, Son. We have to stay with our wagon train. Old Sam Logan will get us through." Andrew said with a hopeful smile.

They started in the late afternoon as it was beginning to cool. When the sun set the wagons took their bearing from the North Star and kept the oxen moving. Andrew and Jake walked beside the wagon to save the oxen and Uncle Dan's horse.

They plodded on into the night and sometime past midnight the wagon stuck fast. Jake could hear the rest of the wagons tinkling and jingling as they continued on. Leather squeaking and men cursing could be heard off in the distance. Soon the sounds grew fainter and fainter until it became still in the cool desert evening.

One of the wheels of the wagon had become bogged down in some sort of a depression. Jake's dad thought they might as well wait until daylight before they did anything about it. They had to be able to see and dawn was only a few hours away.

They got their blankets to keep the night cold out and went to sleep. It was an oddity of the desert that it got so hot during the day and so cold at night. If the heat didn't get you the cold did.

Jake yawned as he came awake. "Well, Dad, what are we going to do?"

"I'm going to pry up the wagon and put something under the wheel, Son. We will be out of here in no time," Andrew said. He began to take apart the wagon tongue to use as a pry bar.

Jake's dad used the wagon tongue as a pry bar and an old stove someone had thrown off to lighten their wagon for a fulcrum. It was working!

Andrew said, "Come over here, Jake, and hold this bar while I pack some dirt under the wheel."

Jake put his weight on the bar and found he could easily hold the bar down even with his light weight. The wagon was up pretty high. The wheel was off the ground and it was just a matter of packing dirt under the wheel and they would be out.

As Andrew crawled under the wagon to pull dirt away from the center of the wagon the fulcrum slipped as the sand shifted. The wagon came crashing down right on top of Andrew. He screamed as he felt ribs snap.

Jake yelled, "Dad! Dad! What should I do?"

"Calm down, Son," Andrew gritted through clenched teeth. "Let's think our way out of this. Get a new position on the stove and try lifting the wagon."

Jake did as he was told and the wagon began to lift off his dad. As he got some room Andrew began to wiggle painfully free. It hurt to move but soon he was out from under the wagon.

Jake got some water for his dad to drink. He bound up his father's ribs as best he could. When he was finished his father coughed and a trickle of blood came out the side of his mouth. Andrew knew he had punctured a lung.

"Son, I'm going to have you go get help. I don't think I can move in the condition I am in," Andrew said.

"Dad! Dad, I can't leave you," Jake cried.

"You have to, Son. You're my only hope," Andrew said weakly.

Jake realized he didn't have any choice. He had to continue on. He left plenty of water and food for his father and packed some for himself.

"Thank you, Son! I want you to know that I love you very much. I am so proud of you. You are a fine son. If I don't make it, I will be with Mom waiting

for you on the other side," Andrew said

as he coughed painfully.

"I'll be back as soon as I can, Dad,"

Jake cried.

As Jake quickly faded from sight

Andrew knew it was the last he would

see of his son on this planet. He could

feel his lungs filling up with fluid and he

knew he would drown in it in a matter of

hours. He had sent his son away

because he didn't want Jake to see him

die. Jake had seen too much death as it

was.

Jake ran as fast as he could in the

hot sun. It wasn't long before he began

to stumble but he kept on. Jake felt his skin redden, then blister. Breathing in the hot desert air was like breathing in a furnace. He kept plodding on for hours it seemed. He kept the sun on his back in the morning and then followed it as it set in the west. As it grew dark Jake fell and passed out from exhaustion and trauma.

Jake didn't know how long he lay there until he felt something kicking his ribs. He woke up with a start. As he looked up he heard a cackling laugh and the person who had kicked him said, "Well, I guess he aint dead after all."

Jake looked up to see a dirty, ragged, huge man grinning down at him.

Jake shouted, "Thank God! I'm so glad you found me! My father is back down the trail a ways and is hurt really bad! Please come help me get him!"

"He aint hurting no more, boy! He's dead!" the smelly man said.

"He didn't mind if I took his wallet and what I could carry off, either" The big, ragged man chuckled.

"NO! You have to be wrong! He's still alive! We have to go back!" Jake cried.

Before Jake could see the man move he slapped him in the face and roared, "Quit sniffling you little snot! You are in my world now!"

"Wha.. what do you mean?" Jake asked in surprise.

"I mean I am going to need a new helper for my mine! And YOU are it!" the gross looking brute yelled with savage delight.

"You can't do that! That's slavery!" Jake shouted.

"The way I figure it, I saved your life and now you are mine!" the dirty man said. "And now I guess I need to give you an attitude adjustment before we start!"

With that the man began to beat him with a leather strap he must have cut off of some reins. Jake didn't know how long the beating lasted. Somewhere in the process he passed out. When he woke up he hurt in every bone in his body. He found he was tied to a travois and was being dragged behind a horse.

They must have been nearly out of the desert because Jake could see a thin line of trees in the distance.

"Well, I'm glad to see I didn't kill you!" the man chucked. "But listen here, Bub! If you don't do what I say I will beat you! You try to leave me and I will hunt you down and kill you. I will feed you and take care of you until you drop or are no good to me anymore. Then I'll cut your throat and leave you in the

desert!" he cackled.

Jake believed him. He couldn't do

anything but stare in shock.

"But the way, my name is Ezra.

What's yours?"

CHAPTER 6

For the next seven years Jake worked like a dog. If he worked too slow, he got kicked. If he caught Ezra in the wrong mood, he got beat. He worked from sun up to sun down digging in the mine, cutting firewood or whatever else was needed. He never got a chance to sneak away and was afraid to try anyway. Ezra never left Jake in a position to escape.

The one good thing about his situation was that he was well fed. Ezra knew that Jake needed food to work hard

– and work hard he did. Digging

tunnels; digging holes; carrying sack of

rock, seemed to be Jakes lot in life.

When supplies got low Jake was

chained in the mine so he could be out of

the sun. Ezra left him with enough food

and water to last him until he returned.

Even if Jake were to escape he would

have probably died in the desert.

Sometimes if it looked like Jake put in an

effort to get free he would get beat when

Ezra got back. Sometime he would pass

out from the pain. Often if the bully was

in a bad mood Jake got a swift kick or a

blow to the side of the head. After a

while Jake developed reflexes where he could avoid most of the blows.

Ezra was a big man. He was tall, much taller than Jake, and wide in the shoulders. But Jake was growing. He could feel it in his bulging muscles as he lifted heavier and heavier sacks of ore. He was getting quick. Most of the time when Ezra took a swing at him he would miss by a large margin. Sometimes he would take two or three swings and Jake would bob and weave to keep from being hit.

Jake could see Ezra watching him with a worried look on his face from time to time. Ezra took to chaining him when he slept.

The day came when Jake moved a little too slowly and Ezra hit him with the belt. Ezra lifted it again and swung but Jake caught it and pulled Ezra toward him. All the anger boiled up in him and he knocked Ezra down.

Ezra jumped up grinning. He had 100 pounds on Jake and he wasn't worried. He was going to beat this kid to death. He swung with a round house punch that would have caved Jakes head in if it would have hit him.

But Jake wasn't there. Everything his dad and his uncle taught him about fighting came back to him. He found that he was much faster than Ezra and just as strong. He darted in and hit Ezra and then darted out before Ezra could lay a hand on him. Before long both Ezra's eyes were closing and blood was running from his nose and mouth. Ezra knew he was in trouble and charged Jake. Jake grabbed Ezra's outstretched arms and threw him over his hip. Ezra landed with a great "whooomp!" He got up slowly.

Jake was getting a great deal of satisfaction out of the beating he was giving Ezra. All the pain and hurt and loneliness somehow connected to those punches. Again and again Ezra charged

Jake. Jake spun around once and kicked Ezra up side his head. When he was getting up Jake kicked him with a mighty kick in his crotch. Ezra fell with a squeal of pain.

Ezra got up and made a stumbling run to get his rifle. Jake tripped him and beat him to it. He cocked it and pointed it at Ezra's middle. Ezra felt to his knees and started blubbering, "Please don't shoot! Please don't shoot!"

Jake didn't shoot but he slammed the butt of the rifle into Ezra's head. Ezra went down instantly and didn't come to until Jake had finished packing himself some food and water. Jake found an old pistol in the cabin. He was well worn and kind of rusty but Jake put it in his belt. He gathered all the ammo he could find for the rifle and pistol. There was quite a lot of it. Ezra must have got it from looting broken down wagons. Jake got a frying pan, coffee pot and all the supplies he thought he would need. He found Ezra hidden stash of money. There was quite a bit of it. Then he turned to Ezra and said,

"By all rights I ought to kill you. You abused me and beat me and made me your slave. But I'm not like you. You can live. I figure all this stuff I am taking is in payment for the work I did for you. If I ever see you again, though, all bets are off. I will kill you where you stand."

With that speech done Jake got on Ezra's horse, took the rope Ezra's mule was tied on and rode toward the setting sun. The stuff he took didn't add up to wages for seven years of hard labor but it would have to do.

Jake didn't know exactly where he was but he figured he would continue to head west. That was the family's goal and now it was his.

Now that he wasn't working from sun-up to sun-down he had time to think – and grieve. He thought of his brother

James and hoped he would have a chance to run into Mean Martin Bigelow someday. He thought of the fight in which his mother and Uncle died. He dwelt on how his father died and was so overcome with grief that he would have cried if he let himself. But a seventeen year old doesn't cry and so he pushed his grief deep down inside his heart and didn't think about it anymore.

Jake found himself in Nevada. It found out it was 1875. People were flocking to Virginia City to work in the mines there. Some people were talking about Bodie, California and Aurora, Nevada. There was excitement in the air.

A young man could find work almost anywhere is he wasn't afraid to sweat.

It was in Virginia City that Jake ran into Martin Bigelow. Bigelow had made a name for himself in the community. He ran with a rough crowd that was thought to be the cause of much of the cities' problems. Men who had a little too much to drink would be hit on the head on the way home and relieved of their gold dust. Someone who won a little too much at the blackjack table, roulette wheel or the poker table would be found shot, knifed, or clubbed. Bigelow's name would often come up as the probable cause. He was known to be a bad man.

As Jake walked through the doors of the Bucket of Blood Saloon he saw Martin the same time Martin saw him. A smile came to Bigelow's face although his eyes were dead and cold.

"Well, if it isn't my old friend, Jake the Snake! Hasn't anyone stomped you yet?" Bigelow sneered.

"A few people tried, but I'm still here," Jake replied. He looked forward with anticipation to the beating he was going to give Martin.

"You aren't back in Minnesota," Martin said. We don't fight with fist out here! We fight with guns. You do have a gun, don't you, Jake?"

Jake still had the old pistol his took from Ezra tucked in his pants. It was rusty and he didn't know if it would even fire. A rifle was his choice of weapons, not a pistol. He hoped it wouldn't let him down.

"I got a gun," Jake said.

The crowd quickly got out of the line of fire as Jake and Martin squared off. Martin was confident. He had killed a number of men in fair gun fights and even more in unfair fights. He was enjoying this moment. He couldn't keep from digging Jake a little before he killed him.

"Remember how I killed your brother?" Martin sneered. "He was sure surprised when that gun went off. You should have seen the look on his face. Then there was the Indian fight with the wagon train. I thought I was a goner when Dan keep saying, "Big… Big…" You thought he was saying you were a big boy but he was trying to say "Bigelow"! Everyone was looking at the Indians. Even Dan would have never know I shot him but I moved a little slow. But it really didn't matter."

"You miserable excuse for a human being. You are lower than scum!" Jake yelled.

"Well draw then!", Bigelow cried as he went for his gun.

Jakes pistol hung up in his pants. He couldn't believe how fast Bigelow was as he yanked to pull his gun.

Jake felt a solid smash to his chest. Another blow knocked his leg out from under him, which was probably a good thing. As he went down another bullet hit him in the head. Everything went black.

CHAPTER 7

When Jake woke up his head was
throbbing. He was in a soft warm bed.
His chest was wrapped in gauze as was
his head and leg. He looked up to see
the most beautiful girl he had ever seen
sleeping in a rocking chair next to his
bed. He thought he must have died and
gone to heaven. Maybe she was an
angel. But he hurt too much for this to
be heaven. He couldn't help it as he
softly he groaned in pain.

The angel must have heard him
move because her eyes fluttered open.

"Who are you? Where am I?" Jake said weakly.

"I am Virginia Ann Palmer and you are in my home sleeping in my bed," the girl said smiling.

"Why? I don't understand. The last thing I remember is getting shot." Jake groaned.

"Indeed, you were shot and would be quite dead except for the Christian Women Temperance Union," Virginia said. "My friends and I came into the Bucket of Blood to protest the selling of alcohol just as that bad man shot you. He calmly walked over to you and would have put a bullet in your brain if we would have let him. My friends and I gathered you up and brought you here to my father's house. He is a pastor of the Methodist Church here in town."

"Th...tha..thank you very much," Jake stammered. "I don't know how I can ever repay you."

"Nobody expects you to pay. We did it for the Lord and His reward is quite enough," Miss Palmer said.

Jake found out he was unconscious for three days. During that time Virginia never left his side, the pastor said. At night she slept in the rocking chair and during the day she hovered over him like an old mother hen.

"I'll bet you must be starving,"
Virginia said.

"YES! I could eat a horse, saddle
and all!" Jake laughed.

Jake couldn't eat much and Virginia
didn't feed him a horse. The homemade
chicken soup tasted like manna from
heaven to Jake.

As the days passed Jake looked
forward to the meals Virginia brought
him. She was so beautiful with red hair
and green eyes. He had never seen
another girl like her. She was so soft and
kind and gentle. Often times she would
sit rocking in the chair and read
Scriptures to him. Sometimes her father

would come and talk to him about the Lord and read the Bible, too. But the only Scripture that filled Jake's heart was "an eye for and eye."

Jake decided that he wouldn't let himself get attached to this beautiful, pure woman when he had vengeance in his heart. Her pure heart made his hard heart seemed so dirty. He had to push impure thoughts from his mind when he saw her beauty and grace. He had never been so attracted to a women in his life.

As soon as he was able he got a room in a cheap hotel. The Palmers tried to talk him out of moving. They protested that he wasn't healed enough.

They tried to talk him out of his anger but he had so much hate in his heart he stubbornly refused all their attempts to change him.

It wasn't that he didn't appreciate everything Virginia and her family did for him. He just had a job to do. He was so grateful to Virginia Ann Palmer but he couldn't stand to be around her when he had such darkness in his heart. He didn't feel worthy of being in her presence.

After a couple of weeks Jake felt good enough to walk around town a little. He tired easily but he was growing stronger. He asked about Bigelow and no one had seen him or his men for weeks. Someone thought they may have gone to Bodie. They were taking a lot of gold out of the ground up there.

Bodie was a rough, tough town. It was said that when someone got up in the morning they would ask, "Did we have a man for breakfast yet?" Usually someone was killed before breakfast every day. Some said it was the wildest and most lawless town in the West.

Jake thought that maybe Bodie was to be his next destination. He knew he didn't have a chance against Bigelow in the physical shape he was in. He also didn't have the skill to meet Martin

Bigelow. He decided he needed to ponder that problem before he did anything or went anywhere.

One day as he was walking around town he walked down to the outskirts of town. He heard some shooting in the distance. As he walked over the hill he saw a group of cowboys shooting pistols. As he watched, they threw bottles in the air, drew their pistols and broke them before they hit the ground.

Someone saw him and waved him over. "Hey, we got an audience," a rough looking cowboy laughed.

Jake was amazed. "That is about the best shooting I have ever seen anyone do with a pistol," Jake said.

"How do you do it?" He asked.

The young cowboy who seemed to be the leader grinned and said, "Practice, practice, practice. That is what we are doing here. Do you want to join us?"

"Sure!" Jake said. "But I don't have a decent pistol."

"You can use one of mine," Curly said. He went to his saddle bags and took out a well-worn pistol. "This is my spare, but you can use it while you practice. It shoots real good." He tossed it to Jake. Jake caught it and looked it over. Jake turned it over in his hands. He remember his training as a youth with guns. He never pointed it at anyone or anything he didn't want to destroy. But he wished he had the opportunity to point it at and destroy one person that came to mind.

Jake spent a couple of weeks with Curly and the boys. They were from Texas and all of them were experts at handling pistols. He learned some fundamentals to shooting a pistol from them. After a while he got pretty good. He wasn't as good as them and he sure wasn't as good as Martin Bigelow, either. That worried Jake.

Jake cleaned up his old pistol and practiced and practiced and practiced some more. He practiced drawing and practiced shooting. He practiced shooting from the hip and with his arm fully extended. He would aim at a target and draw and fire in one swift motion. Lying in his bed he would aim at the clock or a dish and dry fire over and over hundreds of times a day.

One evening as he was walking down Main Street he saw two men in the street. A crowd had gathered and was watching the two men. They both had tied down guns and seemed to be gunfighters. Both of them looked pretty rough and capable.

"Kelly, you lied about me for the last time," one of the men said.

"Are you calling me a liar, boy?" Kelly shouted.

"Yes! You are a liar and a coward to boot!" the young man shouted back.

Kelly drew his pistol so fast that Jake could hardly see the man's hand move. The young man, Jake never found out his name, was fast, too. But he only got his gun clear of his holster when he was shot in the heart. As he went down his arm continued to come up with the gun. Since he had no feeling in his hand to grip the gun, the gun came out of his hand and flew in the air. It landed at Jake's feet.

Jake picked it up and looked it over. It was a new Colt. The action felt smooth as he let the hammer down. Someone with the skill of a watchmaker must have worked on the insides. Jake had never held a gun with such a smooth action.

When the town Marshall came running up everyone agreed it was a fair fight. As some men were packing the body off Jake asked the Marshall, "Hey, Marshall! What should I do with his gun?"

The Marshall shouted over his shoulder, "Keep it! He sure doesn't need it anymore!"

Jake took the forty five caliber pistol home to his room. He took it apart and cleaned it. The pistol was the smoothest operating gun he had ever handled. The trigger pull was dangerously light. The balance was perfect for him. The gun fit in his hand like it was made for it.

Jake loved his new pistol and practiced often but he knew he needed a bigger edge if he was to beat Bigelow. He decided to file the front of the trigger guard off and the front sight as well.

The trigger guard cut out would prevent him from stumbling as he found the trigger. The front sight filed down would keep the gun from hanging up on something. He didn't want any more hang up's like last time.

Jake practiced and practiced. He tried the cross draw. That is where he would put the pistol on the left side of his belt and draw it with his right hand across his stomach. there were two movements to the draw. He had to pull it across his stomach in one motion and then point it toward the target with another motion. If he had the gun in a conventional holster he had to grab the gun, pull it up and point it toward the

target. Two motions again.

Jake thought about it for days. He

thought if he had the gun pointing in the

direction he wanted to shoot he would

eliminate one motion. It seemed there

were two ways to do that. First, he could

have the holster angled in such a way

that it held the gun pointed forward. He

had seen a man with a holster like that

one time. He would only have to pull the

gun and shoot. He tried it a few times

and didn't like how you had to bend

backwards to get the right angle.

Besides, there was a danger of shooting

the holster or his leg. It just didn't feel comfortable or practical to him.

The second way was the one he decided to use. He went to the leathersmith and had him make a special holster to his specifications. He used a hard, thick leather for the holster and had it split in the front. He polished it and waxed it so that there was hardly any friction between the gun and the holster. With the split front he only had one motion. He simply rotated his wrist and the gun popped out on target.

Jake practiced his draw day after day. He got so he was incredibly fast. He could twist his gun out in less than a blink of an eye. He knew he was faster

than any of his cowboy friends, but was

he fast enough? He would know soon

enough. Tomorrow he would go to

Bodie, California. He wouldn't be looking

for gold. He would be looking for

trouble.

CHAPTER 8

Jake got up early, went to the Monarch
Café, where he had gotten in the habit of
eating, and ordered some steak and
eggs. As he was eating he noticed a
couple over in the corner table. The man
was red faced with a scowl on his face.
He was calling the women he was sitting
with filthy names. She hung her head,
embarrassed and afraid. She was
shivering in fear, tears running down her
face.

Jake turned back to his eggs,
determined to stay out of other people's

business. As he lifted his fork he could see the woman pleading with the man.

"Please, Pete! I will do better next time. I didn't mean to make you mad," She whispered.

"Well, you did you skinny, ugly, excuse for a woman!" Pete snarled, and slapped her forcefully along her head. "That ought to get your attention!" he said.

Jake stood up and took a step or two to their table. "That got MY attention, Mister!" Jake spat out, getting angry himself.

"Where I come from a man doesn't treat a woman like that – even if she is his wife." Jake said.

"She aint my wife and this aint your business, Mister! You better butt out before you get hurt." The bully shouted.

"Well I guess we are beyond that," Jake smiled as Pete stood up.

Pete took a swing at Jake and Jake let it sail harmlessly over his shoulder. Jake slapped the angry man across the face with his left hand and then the right. It was so fast it was a blur to the onlookers. The two sounds almost sounded like one.

Pete stepped back with a shocked look on his face. He gritted his teeth and charged Jake like a bull. Jake met the charge, side stepped, and used Pete's momentum to throw him out the front door into the street.

Pete caught his balance before he fell and began to take off his coat. He smiled an evil grin and said, "You got lucky on that one, boy! Now I'm going to hurt you real bad."

The man outweighed Jake by seventy-five pounds and by the scars on his face and hands Jake knew he had some experience in rough and tumble fighting. Someone shouted to Jake,

"Watch him, Mister! He's a mean one!"

Pete rushed at Jake with his arms

open to get him in his grasp where he

would gouge his eyes, bite his nose off or

stomp his heel into his feet if he could.

He had hurt many men before and the

rumor was that he even killed a man

once with his fists and feet.

Jake side stepped and tapped him

with his left to set him up for his right.

As he swung his right he pivoted from his

hips, gaining momentum with the twist,

and landed a tremendous blow to Pete's

jaw. Pete flailed his arms as he landed

on his side in the dust.

He looked up at Jake with gritted teeth and fire in his eyes. "That's gonna cost you, Boy!" He had been in too many fights to let a punch or two discourage him. All he needed was one punch or one kick and he knew the tide would turn.

Pete sprang up with evil intentions on his mind. Before he could get set, Jake was on him like lightening. He hit Pete again and again and then danced out of his reach. Jake flicked a left jab that stung every time it hit. Sometimes he would flick it and snap with his wrist. Other times it would be a hard straight left. Every punch left a mark.

Pete tried rushes, kicks, and every sneaky trick he had up his sleeve but couldn't catch the elusive kid. Again and again Jake punished him.

Jake looked at the bloody man and asked, "Have you had enough?"

"Yeah, I had enough. Let's shake on it." Pete grinned

Jake put out his hand and Pete grabbed it but instead of shaking it he tried to pull Jake toward him. Pete's eyes lit up and his mouth twisted into a cruel grin. "Got you now, you little snake!" Pete said.

Jake twisted the hand Pete grasped toward Pete's thumb, as Uncle Dan had taught him. He lifted his arm upward and broke the grip. As Pete stumbled off balance Jake brought his elbow that was high in the air, back with as much force as he could muster. It landed with a thud on Pete's jaw. As Pete started to fall, Jake's elbow continued on around to Jakes right side in perfect position to swing a mighty right hook to the hinge of Pete's jaw.

Pete landed face first in the dirt. He was out before he hit the ground. He looked totally relaxed and downright peaceful with his hands by his sides and his face slack from his enforced nap.

Someone said, "Looks like he's gonna be sleeping for a while!"

People came up to Jake and started slapping him on the back and congratulating him. "Good going, Boy! Where did you learn to fight like that! Pete had that coming for a long time!"

Jake, trying to get his breath, went back into the Monarch Café. He spied the middle aged, plain-faced woman still in the corner booth crying. As he walked up to her she looked up in surprise.

"Where's Pete?" she asked in astonishment.

"Pete is taking a little nap," Jake grinned. "What's the deal? Why did he hit you?"

"Pete is my brother-in-law. My name is Sarah Mills and my husband died in the mines about a year ago. Pete just moved in and forced me to keep house and cook for him. If I tried to say anything he would beat me. If I told anyone about it Pete would beat them. Everyone was afraid of him when he was home. Fortunately, much of the time he was gone doing whatever he did."

"Well, he won't bother you now," Jake said. "If he does, tell him I will come looking for him and give him a lot worse that he just got just now."

Sarah started crying again and said, "Thank you so much, Mister. I won't ever forget what you did for me."

Jake grabbed his hat, walked down to the stable and started saddling his horse. He figured he had enough money left from the stake he took from Ezra to finance his trip to Bodie if he watched how he spent his money.

The weather was warm and mild as Jake slowly made his way down the mountain trail. When he reached the valley floor he turned south toward Carson City, Genoa, Walker, Bridgeport and then Bodie. It was a nice time of the year with the days warm and the nights cool. Jake stayed in hotels from time to time but usually he preferred to make camp and sleep under the stars.

Eventually Jake came over the dusty road and looked down at a beautiful scenic town with a river running through it on the valley floor. He knew the town was Bridgeport and Bodie wasn't many miles away.

As Jake rode into Bridgeport he pulled up at a new looking hotel called "The Leavitt House". He tied his horse to the rail and walked in the door.

"Can I get a room, please?" he asked the gentleman at the desk.

"Sure, Mister. How many will be staying?" the gentleman asked.

"Just me. How much?" asked Jake.

"A dollar a day or six dollars a week," The hotel owner replied. "Are you going to be staying long?" he asked.

"No," Jake said. "I'm just passing through." He scratched his name in the hotel registry and slid it back across the desk to the clerk who glanced at it.

"Jake King," the clerk said. "Welcome to Bridgeport, formally known as "Big Meadows. I'm Hiram Leavit. I own this humble establishment." "Big

Meadows?" Jake asked with raised eyebrows. "I thought Big Meadows was in Nevada on the east side of the 40 mile desert."

"It is," Hiram said. "But that is Big Meadows, Nevada. This is Big Meadows, California. Wouldn't be surprised if there was another Big Meadows someplace else."

Hiram grinned strangely and slid a key across to Jake. "You have room 16. Should be everything you need there. Outhouse and stable is out back."

"Say, Hiram." Jake asked. "Where could a man pick up a few supplies around here?"

"General store is right across the street. Edwin and Missy Adams own it. They should have everything you need. Where ya headed Young Fella?" asked Hiram in a friendly way.

"I'm going to Bodie." Jake replied.

"BODIE! That's a bad place for a young man like yourself. More than one body rest at the bottom of a glory hole." Hiram warned. "Why do you want to go to such a wicked place?" He inquired.

"I'm looking for a bad man and I figure Bodie is the place to find him," Jake answered.

"Well, you got that right, Jake. There are a lot of bad men, MEAN men there! Just be on your toes." Hiram

warned. "The women are almost as

mean as the men and the weather is

meaner than both of them. Bodie sits on

top of a mountain range above tree line

and more than a few have died from the

cold. Stealing firewood is common in the

winter time and because it could mean

the death of the victim they frown deeply

on such a thing. They hung two guys

last winter over stealing firewood!"

Jake grin and thanked Hiram for

the warning, then found his room. He

had a good night's sleep and felt

refreshed the next morning. As Jake

came down the stairs he was surprised to see Hiram up already.

Hiram looked at him rather strangely and asked, "How did you sleep, Jake?"

"Slept like a log. Couldn't have been better! Why do you ask?" Jake asked a little puzzled.

"Well, a young women hung herself in that room a few years ago." Hiram said. "Her name was Sarah and her husband to be was killed accidentally just before the wedding. Poor Sarah put her wedding dress on and hung herself in room 16. Some people say she still can be seen there from time to time."

Jake laughed and said, "She didn't bother me none.   Maybe she hooked up with her sweetheart. Anyway, she left me in peace."

"Good luck, Jake." Hiram smiled. I hope you find who you are looking for and it ends successfully for you."

"Me, too!" Jake said with a wave.

CHAPTER 9

As Jake left Bridgeport he continued south. Again it was another wonderful mountain day in the Sierras.   The blue lupine flowers gave off a sweet fragrance and the globe mallow with their orange blossoms looked beautiful. It made Jake glad to be alive.

He followed the Walker River south. At noon he stopped in the shade of an aspen tree and dug through his saddlebags. Pretty soon he found his fishing line and hooks. He made a crude pole out of a branch, turned a few rocks over until he found a worm and cast his line in the River. Most places back home in Minnesota they would have called the Walker River a creek. It wasn't very big. Out here it was declared a river.

The water rushed past a large boulder in the middle of river and Jake tossed his line in the calm water on the lee side of the Rock. Instantly something grabbed Jakes line with quite a bit of force. The fish swam into the swift water and Jake thought for sure he would lose him. He didn't, though, even when the fish jumped. Jake could see it was a nice size native speckled Brown trout. Jake eased him to the shore and flipped him onto the rocks. With a swift thump with a rock the fish stopped flopping around. Jake cleaned him and fried him in his old cast iron frying pan with a little bacon grease and salt. He thought it was about the best lunch he ever had.

After he scrubbed out his pan with some sand from the creek and rinsed it with cold mountain water he packed it away again. Before he got on the trail again he practiced his draw a hundred times and dry fired another hundred. He was getting fast and smooth at snapping his gun up. Instead of extending it to arm's length like most of the cowboys did he practiced shooting from the holster. It was kind of iffy past 10 or 15 yards but if he needed it in a hurry it would be at close quarters anyway. At long range he had his rifle. He just needed to get close enough for his speed and accuracy to be a factor.

Jake put his pistol in his hard black holster, hooked the leather loop over the hammer to keep it secure and stepped into his saddle. Before dark he came to a place called Willow Springs. He decided to camp there.

As he came to the spring he saw someone else was camped there. He shouted, "Hello the camp! Can I come in?"

"Sure, Pilgrim! Come right on in," a voice bellowed from the willows.

Jake slowly came to the campfire. Someone had been cooking some beans, Jake saw. A dirty, ragged looking man, Jake took to be a miner, stepped out with a smaller, but equally dirty man beside him.

"Well, lookee, lookee here, Bartholomew! We got us a young fella headed for the gold fields! Wonder if he got himself a stake!" the miner said with a lecherous look on his face.

The hair on Jakes neck stood up and he knew he was in trouble. "Look, Mister. I don't want any trouble. I just thought I would camp under those trees over there," Jake said pointing with his chin.

"Oh, there won't be any trouble," The big one said. "Will there Bartholomew?"

"No, Zeke! Won't be any trouble at all. There are two of us and only one of him! Won't be any trouble at all." Bartholomew laughed.

Zeke grinned and calmly said, "Look, young fella. We are miners and we need a grubstake. We aim to take yours."

Jake grinned back at him and said, "No, I don't think so. You fellas grab your stuff! Pack up and ride off. I aim to camp here and I don't want to watch my back while you are around."

"Woooooeeee, Zeke! Did you hear that?" Bart shouted.

"Smart-alecky little guy, aint he!" Zeke growled in a low voice.

Jake stepped away from his horse and toward Bart and Zeke. When he was about ten feet away he said, "Look! You got a choice. You can leave peaceful – right NOW! Or you can fill your hand."

Jake's confidence disturbed the pair a little bit but there were two of them. Both went for their guns at the same time! Jake pushed the heel of his hand down on the butt of his gun and it snapped up in line with the chest of the smaller of the pair. Jake figured the small one was the faster of the two – and he was right. Bartholomew's gun started to lift when Jake shot him in the chest. Jake's gun continued on to his left and he thumbed back the hammer and shot Zeke between the eyes. As he was falling Jake shot him in the chest and went back to Bart. Bart was falling to his knees trying to line his gun up when Jake shot him in the head.

Jake was quaking with the rush of adrenalin coursing through his body. That was too close for comfort. He hated to kill the pair of miners but he knew he had no choice. Even if he would have ridden off he knew they would have come for him in the middle of the night.

Jake lifted the pair on their mule and took them to a gully he had pasted a ways back, threw them into it and caved the bank down on them to bury them.

Jake went back to the camp and finished eating their beans, curled up in his blanket and tried to get some sleep.

In the morning he packed up and rode into Dog town. It was a small community of tents and weathered buildings. It had once been a thriving boomtown but it was clearly petering out.

Jake rode up to a tent that said "Red Eye Saloon" on it. He flipped his reins over the hitching post and went inside. There was a card game going on in the corner and one gambler was playing solitaire hoping for someone to come play blackjack. He looked hopefully at Jake.

Jake shook his head and said, "I just came in for a little information."

Jake knew that the saloon was the hub of information in any community. Men were worse gossips that women and if anything was going on they would know about it.

"Say, Mister!" he asked the bartender as the barkeeper wiped greasy glasses. "How far to Bodie from here?"

The bartender scrunched up his face in thought and said, "It about a day's ride east of here. You go up the canyon just east of town and the road climbs up for about ten miles and you will hear the stamp mills and see the smoke before you come to it. You can't miss it!"

Jake walked out and found a hotel and got a room for the night. It wouldn't be long now. He threw his saddle bags on the bed, leaned the chair against the door under the doorknob and began to practice drawing his pistol again.

Jake slept well after the previous night's sleeplessness and was up well before dark. He found the tent that served as a café, had eggs, fried potatoes and salt pork for breakfast. He found his horse and headed east toward Bodie.

The trip was just as the bartender said. Jake could hear the stamp mills from miles away. He could feel the ground shake. He wondered how anyone could get used to that. They did, though. He heard someone say that when they left Bodie they actually missed the hammering and noise.

Jake topped the ridge and looked down at the town of Bodie, California. It was the baddest town of the bad towns in the entire Wild West. He could see a church off to one side of the town and a graveyard beyond that. He could see a huge mill over on the other side of the valley and the main street had to be a mile long. It had every kind of store and bar imaginable. Jake breathed a little prayer through gritted teeth as he descended to the town, "Lord, help me! Forgive me for what I am about to do?"

As Jake reached the town he saw dozens of saloons and gambling halls, all seemed to be thriving businesses. He decided he better find a room and settle in. He found a boarding house run by a motherly older woman name Mary Ellen Anderson. The stable was out back and Fred, Mary Ellen's husband put up his horse. The food was plentiful and good. When Jake was done he hitched up his gun belt and decided to check the town out.

Jake was astonished at the amount of people and the number of businesses.

At this time of year it was real pleasant to stroll around town. He was continually on guard lest he run into Martin Bigelow. He didn't want to give him any advantage the next time they met.

Jake saw miners, ranchers, storekeepers and people of every kind and nationality. He saw saloon girls and houses of ill repute that were willing to pleasure any man –IF he had the gold dust to pay for their services. He saw saloons and opium dens that promises to help a man forget all his troubles. What he didn't see was a Marshall's office. He stopped someone on the street and asked where it was at. He was directed to Sheriff Dan McMillian, the one armed sheriff of Mono County.

As Jake stepped into the Sheriff's office the man sitting behind the desk with one sleeve pinned up asked, "What can I do for you, Young Fella?"

Jake eyed the one armed man. It was said that he was the manager of the town baseball team and he looked quite capable in spite of his handicap. "I'm looking for a man, sir. I was hoping you could tell me if he is here."

"Sure, Son," Sheriff McMillian answered. "What's your friend's name?"

"He isn't my friend, that's for sure. If I find him I plan to kill him. He killed my brother and my uncle," Jake scowled. "He goes by the name of Bigelow, Martin Bigelow."

"Oh boy! You chawed off a big chunk with that one, Son!" the sheriff frowned. "That is one mean son of a gun! He killed three men since he came here. He never gave them a chance but no one will testify against him."

"That sounds like him", Jake said. "You sure don't want to turn your back on him. Where can I find him?"

"He was hanging out at McAlister Saloon most of the time. I haven't seen him for a couple of days," The Sheriff said. "Don't start anything you can't finish, Mr. King. Our graveyard is already pretty full."

"You can count on that, Sheriff!" Jake said as he headed for the door.

Jake found McAlister's Saloon halfway down the next block. He unlatched his pistol and made sure it was free. He glanced through the window and didn't see anyone who resembled Bigelow. As he looked over the batwing doors he could see a couple of cowboys pushing a miner around. Jake stepped in and looked around and didn't see any sign of Bigelow.

Just then one of the cowboys
pushed the miner and the other one
tripped him. The dusty miner fell into
Jake.

Jake pushed him off and said,
"Hey, watch it you two!"

"What are you going to do about it,
Slim?" one of the cowboys asked.

Jake slapped him in the mouth with
his right hand in a blur of speed. The
cowboy brought his gun up and with his
left hand Jake grabbed the gun. His
right hand held a cocked forty five
revolver to the man's face.

The cowboy went white faced as he
realized how close to death he was. He

stuttered, "I, I, I'm, sorry, Mister! I didn't mean nothin'. We were just funnin' with ol' Bill here."

Jake looked at the other cowboy and the young rider put his hands up in a sign of defeat. "I don't want any part of this, Stranger! We didn't mean nothin'" he swallowed.

Jake took the gun from the first cowboy's hand and gave it to the bartender. "Keep this until tomorrow," Jake said as he holstered his gun.

The two cowboys scrambled out of the bar as quickly as they could. "Jumpin' Jehoshaphat! That was the fastest I have ever seen a man pull a hog leg! And I have seen 'em all!"

The miner exclaimed. "Thanks, Mister, you saved my bacon for shore!"

"You're welcome", Jake said. I hate to see an unfair fight. My name's Jake King, by the way."

"Mine's Jethro Miller. Hey, Jake! How would you like to work for me? I own a pretty good paying mine but I can't get any ore to the mill. I need a guard who could take it from my mine to the mill."

"I shore need the money, Jethro," Jake said, "but I got a job to do. I'm looking for a man by the name of Martin

Bigelow. When I find him I'm going to kill him or die trying!"

"Hey, Jake!" The bartender said as he listen in on the conversation. "Bigelow and his bunch headed to Candelaria last week. They had something big they were cooking up."

"Well, Jethro, I guess you hired yourself a guard. I need the money and I am glad to help you at the same time," Jake said as he held out his hand.

For the next month Jake earned what he considered to be a lot of easy money. He didn't know if it was because he was riding shotgun or because Bigelow and his boys were out of town.

Whatever the reason was, Jethro got load after load to the mill and paid Jake off in gold dust.

After the job was done Jethro pointed Jake in the direction of Aurora, another rip roaring mining town about ten miles east of Bodie. When Jake rode into town he was impressed with all the brick buildings. Aurora seemed like a prosperous town that planned to stay awhile. Jethro said they had made it the county seat of Mono County, California. Now they were saying it was really in Nevada. Jake didn't know what to believe, but it was a pretty place with a stream running through the middle of town.

Jake only stayed one night. He got directions and headed to Candelaria. He filled his canteens at Fletcher. Water came directly out of solid rock in the desert floor. It reminded him of Moses and the rock in the wilderness. A touch of nostalgia flood him as he recalled how Uncle Dan could make those stories come alive.

Jake rode up Lucky Boy pass, and when he went down went down the other side he could see Walker Lake to the north. He camped at Whiskey Flat, so called because of the reddish burgundy, and noon found him at Rattlesnake wells. He knew it wasn't much farther to Candelaria. He burned with rage as he thought about that meeting with Martin Bigelow in Virginia City. He remembered how Bigelow laughed at him and bragged to him about killing his brother James and his Uncle Dan. Bigelow thought he had Jake that time. It was a different Jake King that hunted him today than the one whom Martin shot and would have left for dead if that little band of religious women hadn't protected him. He wondered if he would ever see Virginia Ann Palmer again. He sure hoped so.

Jake finished his lunch and began to practice his draw.

10 CHAPTER NAME

Candeleria was another mining town in the middle of nowhere. It was in the high desert sage. Once a person got to the outskirts of town there was nothing but sagebrush and shrubs for miles in every direction. It was actually quite beautiful. The sage gave it a bluish tint and the ground had a lot of color to it from a burgundy color the iron ore in it gave it to the bluish green color that copper ore gave. Only gold or silver would draw a man to a place like this – or the attraction of taking other men's gold from them. Jake's pull was the hope of finding a man he wanted to kill.

As Jake pulled into town he looked for a place to water his horse. They were both a little dry. He stopped in front of the Red Dog Saloon and stepped down. Out front was a watering trough for his horse but it was empty of water. A sign said he could get water inside for one dollar a gallon. He climbed down, grabbed his saddle bags and went inside.

He stepped up to the bar and asked the bartended where a good hotel was and how come water was so high.

The bartender laughed and said, "I guess that would be in Reno, if you are looking for a good hotel. But if you aren't too picky there's one down the street a ways. And the reason the water is so high is because it has to be hauled ten miles. There aint any water any closer."

"Okay," Jake said. "Give me a gallon of water for my horse and another one for me."

After Jake watered his horse and filled his canteen he went back inside and asked the barkeep if he knew a man by the name of Martin Bigelow. The man turned red and an angry look came on his face.

"Yeah, I know him. He wore out his welcome here. He and his friends busted up my bar and killed a man right where you a standing. The poor guy didn't have a chance. Two of his men got on either side of him and then Bigelow braced him. When he went for his gun the guy on his right grabbed his gun as it come up and Bigelow shot him full of holes. They say the old boy had just found a glory hole full of pure gold. Bigelow owes it now. Got the paper and everything. Legal as can be."

"Thank you, Mister. I'll go find that hotel now," Jake said.

As he turned to go the saloon man said after him, "If you are looking for Bigelow you can probably find him at the "Oasis Saloon" down the street. He has been hanging out there lately."

Jake decided he might as well get this over with. He had been following him for so long the quest had consumed his life. All he lived for was to find Bigelow and kill him. He had imagined it in every way possible. Beating him to death with his fists, ripping his guts out with a knife, shooting him a variety of ways, just to name a few. He thought of killing Martin's horse, dog or anything he valued, before he killed Bigelow. Jake realized that he had become a killer and a hater and he didn't like what he saw in himself.

Jake, hitched up his gun belt and determined to get it over with. Tonight it would be over. Either he or Mean Martin Bigelow would be dead – or maybe both of them.

The sun was setting as Jake walked into the Oasis Saloon. The sun was shining on his back as he stepped through the bat wing door. Jake instantly saw Bigelow sitting against the back wall. Martin glanced up at Jake but all he could see was an outline of a man.

The face was dark and the form was outlined by the setting sun.

The figure took a step toward Bigelow and Bigelow jerked with a start. "Jake King! I thought I killed you!" he said.

Jake said, "You almost did. It took me a while to heal up. But now I am here to make you pay for what you did to my family."

Bigelow stood up and said, "This time I will make sure you stay dead. There aren't any little church girls to save you this time."

Patrons of the saloon slowly got up and backed out of the line of fire. An old trapper with a long curly cue moustache close to Jake at the bar lifted his scatter gun up and said, "Boy's let's have us a fair fight. Ol' Trapper Joe will make sure it's fair. Go ahead, Young Man. Do what you got to do."

"Thanks, Mister. I owe you one." Jake said with one eye on Martin.

"You don't owe me a thing, Jake. Yeah, I recognized your name! Your Uncle Dan and I did a little trapping together before the war. He saved my hair more than once. And you tell me this scallywag killed him? I don't believe it! Dan was better than that!"

"It's true," Jake said. It happened in an Indian fight. While Dan was shooting at the Paiutes ol' Martin here shot him in the back. He bragged on it to me in Virginia City."

"I shot you then and I will shoot you now!" Bigelow yelled and went for his gun.

He was fast! He was really fast! But Jake had put in too many hours practicing his draw. Truth be told, Martin was as fast as Jake, maybe even a little faster, but Martin had to lift his gun from his hostler, level it, and point it to shoot –two motions. Jake just twisted his gun up in one smooth motion. Before Martin could make the second motion to shoot Jake, Jake was fanning the hammer of his Colt. The first shot caught Bigelow in the throat. The next two took him in the heart. The last shot went right between his eyes. Mean Martin Bigelow crashed backwards, sat in his chair, and slowly fell over to the dirty sawdust floor.

Jake stared in shock. He couldn't believe it was over. Ol' Joe slapped him on the back and said, "That was some right fine shooting, Boy. You did your Uncle proud!"

Whoever Bigelow's friends were didn't let it be known. It was said that a few hard cases slipped out of town that

night and headed west. Jake had a drink
with Joe but was too upset to eat
anything. Joe told a couple of tall tales
about his Uncle that Jake had never
heard before. After a while he slipped
away from the old trappers company and
got his horse and rode toward Tonopah
Springs. Jake rode for half the night
before he got sleepy enough to make
camp. He slept soundly for a couple of
hours and woke as the sun rose in the
eastern sky.

He skipped breakfast and mounted
up and rode toward the rising sun. It
wasn't very long before he could see

some trees in the distance. He knew it was Tonopah Springs.

As he rode he thought of his family. They had started out so optimistic and full of dreams and hope. But life had cut them down – all but himself. He was alone again, but this time he had no purpose, no mission, and no agenda. He faced reality. He was a warrior. He was a killer. He had changed. Life had changed him – and not for the good.

Life seemed so painful. He thought that maybe his parents, brother and uncle were the lucky ones. Life was so unbearably painful. "Maybe a person was better off dead," he thought.

Then an angelic face came to his mind. A little red-headed, Christian girl's face. His thoughts turned to the little warrior who fought demon rum and the sins of the flesh with the WCTU. He remember his father's prayers and the bible stories Uncle Dan told. He wondered if there would be a place for a man like him among that worthy group. He decided when he got to a town he would see if he could find her. He doubted if she would want a man like him but it was worth a try. He heard there was a little town called Los Vegas south of where he was. Maybe he would

take a gamble and start his search there.

ABOUT THE AUTHOR

Andy was born in Northern Minnesota but moved to Montana at a young age. Hungry Horse, Whitefish, Colombia Fall, and Neihart were some of the places he called home in Montana. In Minnesota home was (and is) a little town called Wirt, formally known as "Rattlesnake" because it was so wild. His grandfather was constable during some of those wild years.

Grossman has been a logger, iron mine worker, insurance investigator, Minuteman Missile Weapons System Mechanic, Correctional Officer and pastor. He joined the U.S. Army in the Viet Nam era and was a Military Policeman and dog handler in Korea. He achieved the rank of Sargent.

Grossman spent time as a youth in the ghost towns of Montana and later spent 13 years living in Nevada where he was able to visit all the old ghost towns there and later when he moved to California he was able to investigate some of the ghost town there.

Andy says that he has had a 'western novel' brewing in the back of his mind for years. Recently he sat down and decided to bring it to life. His first novel, "The Making of a Killer" is the result.